First published by Rising Spirit; Where Great Ideas Grow
in 2023, Perth, WA, Australia

This edition published in 2023

A catalogue record for this is
available from the
National Library of Australia

www.alyssacurtayne.com

ALYSSA CURTAYNE

Yexian

The Chinese Cinderella

Issue 1

Contents

05
RETELLING

13
STORY HISTORY

16
TRANSLATED SUMMARIES

19
SYMBOLS AND MOTIFS

21
CREATIVE REIMAGINING

INTRODUCTION TO YEXIAN

This story is a Cinderella variant found first in southern China in the 9th century. The exact origins of the story are not known and academics are still exploring the possibilities, including the possibility that it evolved independently of the European Cinderella or was influenced by it. It's possible we might never know.

This project began as storytelling research for a performance, but so much information was available deep in academic papers that I decided that others might be interested in the story's origins in an easy-to-read format. It is my hope that this book can be used by storytellers and researchers as a start-point for their explorations of this fabulous story of hope in the darkness, of the possibilities for us to re-imagine what we understand Cinderella to be and its relevance for us today.

I hope in these pages you learn something new or have a new appreciation for Yexian and the Cinderella tale, either in folktale or fairytale. Either way, I've loved every minute of creating this for you. Enjoy!

一妻卒有女名葉限少惠善陶
父卒為後母所苦常令樵險汲
餘頳鬐金目遂潛養於盆水日
受乃投於後池中女所得餘食
魚必露首枕岸他人至不復出
未嘗見也因詐女曰爾無勞乎
其弊衣後令汲於他泉計里數
女衣袖利刃行向池呼魚魚即
長丈餘膳其肉味倍常魚藏其
女至向池不復見魚矣乃哭於
自天而降慰女曰爾無哭爾母
爾歸可取魚骨藏於室所須第
其言金璣衣食隨欲而具及洞
女伺母行遠亦往衣翠紡上衣

IMAGE TEXT: FROM LOUIS, 1982

YEXIAN

A version written by Alyssa Curtayne based upon the existing English translations as outlined in this book

You may have heard of this charming tale, but you may not have heard the version that I am going to share with you today. It has influenced fairy tale and cultures across centuries and continues to be one of the most re-told stories in the world today. I invite you to imagine, a time, in the dim past, well before the dynasties there lived a people in the far south of China, in a village, set in the caves of the hills. Their chief was an elder named Wu. As a young man, Wu had been a natural leader who had fought in some fierce battles, but now, moved into a life of domesticity and took a wife. His wife, bore him a daughter, Yexian. Not long after, her mother died. Wu took a second wife, who bore him another daughter, Jun-Li. He was harsh, but fair with his daughters, but Yexian was intelligent, and brought him much wealth on the wheel so, he favoured her over Jun-Li.

After some years, Wu died. Yexian felt very alone in the world. The moment her father was buried, her stepmother stripped her of her fine clothing and made her sleep by the hearth. In the morning, her stepmother would throw the bucket at her and tell her to fetch water from the deepest well, a half-day walk from the village. When she returned, her stepmother would order her into the most dangerous parts of the forest to collect firewood. Then Yexian would fall into a deep, dreamless sleep before the day would start again. Yexian dreamed of spinning on the wheel and seeing her father's kindly face. Jun-Li and Yexian had been close before their father died, but after his death, Jun-Li ordered her older sister to do jobs, just as her stepmother did.

Once, just after her father died, Yexian was collecting water from a deep well when she came across a stream. She stripped her tattered clothing off and hung them on a branch. Then checking her modesty, submerged her aching body into the water. The gentle current caressed her free-flowing hair as she lay facing the blue sky. Something brushed against her. She sat up and looked about her. It was a fish, about as long as her finger, with red fins and a magnificent set of whiskers that reminded her of her father's long moustache. She cupped it in her hands, and it seemed as though it were speaking to her through its round, golden eyes. Perhaps her fortune would turn around, after all these fish were a sign of prosperity, luck and abundance. She squatted on a rock to dry Yexian spoke to it about her troubles and watched the fish swim in circles near her feet as if it were listening. Remembering the time and her stepmother's punishments, she dressed. She picked up her buckets of heavy water and looked at the fish. For the first time she didn't feel alone.

"Would you like to come with me?" she asked. It seemed that her new friend wanted to. She placed it in one of the buckets. At home, she found a small, broken bowl on the dung heap and washed it, being careful to not let her stepmother or sister see her. Then placed the fish carefully in the bowl and put it under her bed. Every day would speak to it and bring whatever food she could find. It grew so quickly she soon needed a new bowl for it. Months went by and the fish was now as long as her arm and she knew she would need to move it. She found a secluded pond, wedged in-between a cliff face and in a rare moment of privacy, she carried it there.

The pond had a sandy edge and when the fish saw Yexian's tattered clothing it pillowed itself on the bank and listened to her talk while she fed it. It was soon about three metres long. Yexian fell into a daily routine and for a while it seemed as though she and her fish lived in a bubble of friendship and love. One morning, when her stepmother had been particularly cruel, Yexian didn't take her usual precautions to keep her fish friend hidden. Jun-Li followed her and hid behind the rocks that bordered the pond. She heard Yexian lamenting her stepmother's cruelty and watched her feed it bread. Jun-Li returned to her mother and told her everything. The stepmother was furious that Yexian had kept a secret from her but didn't say anything to her about it and told Jun-Li that she would fix it.

A month passed and life continued as normal. The stepmother called Yexian to her: "Girl, you must go and collect water from the spring near the neighbouring village."
"Yes, stepmother," Yexian replied, putting on her cloak.
"No, you cannot wear those clothes to the village, you will bring shame to the Wu family," she said, thrusting a new coat at her.

As soon as Yexian had gone, she put on Yexian's tattered cloak, tucked a sharp blade up her sleeve and followed Jun-Li to the pond and bade the girl to wait outside. The stepmother called to the fish as Yexian had done and when it recognised the tattered clothing, it pillowed its head on the sandy bank. The moment it did, the stepmother raised the blade above her head and swiftly cut off its head. She then called to Jun-Li and together they carried the heavy body of the fish home to their cottage. Without hesitation, the two prepared the fish and had a most satisfying dinner. By the time Yexian returned home, it was dark and she was exhausted.

It wasn't until the following afternoon when Yexian had the opportunity to go to the pond. She was excited to see her friend, but when she arrived, her fish didn't appear. All that was left was its beautiful head, the whiskers curled in on themselves. Yexian fell to her knees in the sand and howled with grief. Tears fell into the still waters, creating a ripple across its surface. In the water's reflection, a light appeared. Yexian turned to find a glowing being behind her. They were aged with long, white hair over their shoulders and kindly face, despite their coarse clothes.

"Your stepmother has killed your fish and its bones are under the dung heap," they put a hand on her shoulder. "The fish's bones are filled with a powerful spirit. Whatever your heart's desire, you have only to kneel before them and ask and it is bound to be granted." Without another word, the sage returned to the sky.

Yexian followed their advice and retrieved the bones from the dung heap. She dug through rotting food scraps, ashes from the hearth, and the remains of the chamber pot until she found every bone. Yexian returned to the sacred pond and carefully washed each bone. She used a scrap of her father's old shirt to wrap them in and hid them under her pillow. From then on Yexian was able to kneel before the bones and provide herself with simple things that she desired whenever she wanted them. Now she had seen her stepmother's capabilities, she took more care not to draw attention to herself. She submitted and did exactly as her stepmother instructed.

Life continued in this way until the blossoms emerged from their sleeping. It was time for the annual festival. This was a celebratory time of the year when everyone came together to reconnect, tell stories, trade and arrange marriages.

“You will not be coming,” her stepmother ordered. “Watch over the fruit trees for thieves,” she said taking Jun-Li with her.

Yexian complied, but as soon as they had passed out of sight, Yexian went to her pillow, extracted her precious bones, and knelt before them.

“Deliver me a disguise so I may be able to attend the festival,” she said.

Within moments, she was clad in an iridescent cloak of kingfisher feathers. On her feet were slippers, woven in gold threads in a pattern like the scales of a fish, and the glistening soles were made of solid gold. Although they should have been heavy, when she walked her feet felt as light as air. Yexian thanked the fish bones and returned them to their hiding place and made her way to the festival.

Yexian radiated with the bones of the fish and shone like a light at the festival, making many connections. But nearing sunset, when her feathers glistened off the sun’s rays, she overheard Jun-Li say: “Mother, doesn’t that look like our Yexian?”

“Yes, it does, daughter,” she replied.

Yexian’s heart sank and she inhaled deeply, trying to remain calm. She turned the other direction as calmly as possible. As soon as she was out of sight, Yexian raced down the mountainside and in doing so, lost a slipper. She was in such a panic she didn’t notice until she arrived home in her tattered clothing.

She placed the remaining slipper under the pillow with the bones, but the bones of the fish no longer spoke to her. The magic was gone. In her distress, Yexian went into the garden and wrapped her arms around one of the fruit trees, and sobbed herself to sleep. In the morning she was awakened by a bucket.

But what of the slipper? It was picked up by one of the people of the village, who sold it to a merchant. The village was near an island. On this island was a nearby kingdom. Its king was powerful and ruthless. The merchant, seeking the king's favour, gave the shoe to the king. The king was entranced by its magic, lightness, and fine workmanship. He told those about him to put it on, but when they did, it shrunk. He ordered all the women in his kingdom to try it, but there was not one that it fitted. The king coveted the magic of the shoe and wanted its matching pair. He went through homes and arrested people if there was a woman's shoe found. Soon the king came to the house of Wu and after trying the stepmother and stepsister, he searched the inner-rooms and found Yexian. He made her put it on. She then came forward with both shoes and was cloaked in magic in her gown spun from kingfisher feathers. She radiated with the spirit of the bones of the fish and felt complete once again.

But this is not the end of the story, and it doesn't end with a happily ever after. The king ordered Yexian to tell him how she came to possess the magic shoes and cloak. Reluctantly she told him about the magic fish bones. He took Yexian and the bones back to his kingdom. Yexian never saw her stepmother or stepsister again. They were rumoured to be killed in a landslide after a terrible storm and Yexian felt more alone than ever. She hoped that with both shoes back together, the fishbone spirit would again speak to her, but the bones were silent.

The king used the bones for himself and made Yexian his chief wife because she had made him so rich. The king's greed had no bounds, in the first year the king got pearls, gold, and jade without limit. Yexian hoped to reunite with her bones, but the king kept them well hidden until all his enemies learned about their power.

In an attempt to hide the bones, one night, the king buried them on the banks of the river. In the darkness, Yexian heard the call of the bones and the spirit of her friend again. She crept to the shore and on her knees spoke to the bones. She was overjoyed to be reconnected with her friend. They invited her to lie down beside them and she slept. During the night, the tide rose and the bones and Yexian were washed into the current. Yexian was finally reunited with her beloved friend once again.

"

SHE RADIATED WITH THE SPIRIT OF BONES OF THE FISH AND FELT COMPLETE ONCE AGAIN

ALYSSA CURTAYNE

STORY HISTORY

THE ORIGINS OF YE XIAN

Although we may never discover the true origins, the very first documented Cinderella-type tale comes from China.

There are reports that stories of a Cinderella character and the shoe/sandal/slipper originate in either Ancient Egypt or Ancient Greece and Anderson puts forward a compelling argument in his book, *Fairytale in the Ancient World*. But this work is not to argue this point, but to put forward the importance of "the earliest exemplar of the story" Yexian (Mair, p. 363) which likely originates in Indigenous peoples of southern China in 221-207 BCE, "before the Qin (221–207 BCE) and Western Han (206 BCE –6 CE) dynasties" (Mair, p. 3660).

During the Qin period, Chinese officials were appointed to collect, "investigate and report upon the legends, folk tales and anecdotes current among people" (Edwards, E.D., 1974). One of the most recognised collections, The Miscellaneous (or smorgasbord) Record of Yu Yang* was by Duan Chengsui (Yu Yang Tsa Tsu/Tuan Ch'eng-Shih) who lived from 800-863CE. This collection contains

Yexian. Mair (p. 363) reports a legend that during "burning of the books" by the Qin Emperor, where scholars sought refuge and stored books in a cave on the mountain and that place, "Youyang came to signify rare and old books from far away."

The record contains 1300 anecdotes "of legends...reports on natural phenomena, short anecdotes and tales of the wondrous and mundane." The author had "a great zest for acquiring out-of-the-way information" (Waley, p. 226) and "a particular penchant for all things arcane, strange and alien" (Mair, p. 363). Duan Chengsui was the son of an official who managed the "aborigines of the south," (see Reed for more about this). While the exact location of the story is unknown, there were reports that the Zhuang peoples were "culturally and socially, this part of the empire was almost completely un-Chinese" (Mair, p. 363) and in the early stages of the Chinese empire and therefore distinct.

The Cinderella story itself is to have believed to travel across the Silk Road and trade routes in both directions and across class groups, leaving elements of the story behind for other interpretations. But it was not until it was written in Giambattista Basile's Pentamerone: Tale of Tales in 1634 that 'Cinderella' as we know it today was first recorded in Europe. From there it inspired the writers of the French Salons including Madame D'Aulnoy (Finette Cendron) and Charles Perrault (The Little Glass Slipper) before being picked up by the Grimm Brothers as Aschenputtel. Folklorists classify it under the ATU index as Magical Tales 510A (Persecuted Heroine). There are believed to have more than 350 variants of the story as recorded by folklorist Marian Roalfe Cox in 1893, followed up in Heidi Ann Heiner's collection in 2012. Of course, Cinderella remains one of the most retold stories in the world today and was told as a film by Walt Disney in 1950. Subsequently, there have been too many retellings to list here.

Yexian itself was not translated into English until 1932 by Jameson (Zhang, p.1) then in 1947 by Waley, and in 1982 Ai Ling Louis used a version from Hsueh Chin T'ao Yun (1644-1912). However, since it is a later version, European sensibilities, including the romantic ending, could have influenced it. You can see in the summaries, particularly the end, how the Louis version diverts from the original translations. Mair's translation in 2005 introduced some new concepts not clear in previous translations including: Yexian is an older sister, the shoe shrinks when tried on by others, the spirit messenger is not identified as either man or woman and rather than spinning on the pottery wheel, she's spinning gold for her father, that's why he loves her so.

XE XIAN

timeline

I really wanted this to be the original roots of Cinderella, however there is insufficient evidence to say so. However, it is "the earliest exemplar of the story" (Mair, p. 363)

221-207BCE — The story is set "before the Qin (221–207 BCE.) and Western Han (206 BCE –6 CE) dynasties," (Mair, p. 366)

221-220AD — China appointed officials 'to investigate and report upon the legends, folk tales and anecdotes,' Edwards, E.D., 1974.

850-860AD — The Miscellaneous Record of Yu Yang

1634 — Oldest known European version of Cinderella by Giambattista Basile in *The Tale of Tales*

1697 — Charles Perrault's Cinderella/The Little Glass Slipper in *Old Time Tales*

1932 — Jameson's first English Translation of Yeh-hsien

1947 — Arthur Waley's translation and analysis of Yeh-hsien

1950 — Walt Disney's animation of Cinderella

1982 — Ai Ling Louis' translation of the Hsueh Chin Tao Yun's 1644-1912 into a picture book, Yeh Shen.

SUMMARIES

ARTHUR WALEY, 1947

- A daughter of a village elder was born
- Her step-mother treated her poorly
- She found a golden-eyed fish and helped it grow, then put it in the pond
- The fish was her friend and hid from everyone else
- The stepmother tricked the girl, killed the fish, and dished it up.
- The girl was heartbroken about the loss of her fish, a sky man came and told her the bones were magic and could provide all she needed.
- Cave festival came (marriage opportunities), Yeh-hsien was left behind. She used the bones to dress herself. Her step-sister recognised her and she ran away leaving a shoe.
- The shoe was taken by a villager, he sold it and the ruler of T'o-han got it.
- Yeh-hsien was asleep with her arms around a tree when the step-mother got home
- The ruler of T'o-han ruled all women to try the shoe on and imprisoned the villager because he thought he got it unlawfully.
- The ruler went through houses and arrested people until he found Yeh-hsien and made her put on the shoe.
- She came forward dressed as a heavenly being.
- She served the king, he took her and the fish-bones back to his kingdom.
- The step-mother and sister were killed in a rockfall. It was then called Tomb of the Distressed Women.
- The king made Yeh-hsien his chief wife, she missed the fish-bone spirit
- The king buried the bones on the sea shore and they got washed away. It's unknown what happens to Yeh-hsien.
- This story was told to me by one of the men of the village who remembers many strange things about the South.

AI LING LOUIS, 1982

- Begins with translation details – suggests story originates from Asia.
- Southern cave chief called Wu, had two wives, one died. Not long after Wu died too.
- Yeh-Shen's stepmother jealous of beauty and goodness compared to her own daughter. Gave her difficult chores.
- Yeh-Shen's only friend a fish she fed and raised. Stepmother heard of it, but the fish hid itself.
- Stepmother tricked Yeh-Shen into leaving her coat behind and the stepmother hid a dagger in her sleeve, stabbed fish, wrapped it and took it home to cook for dinner.
- Yeh-Shen discovers missing fish. Tears into pond.
- Old man tells her of the fish's manner of death and power of spirit in the bones.
- She retrieves the bones and takes comfort in speaking to the bones of the fish and asks for food secretly.
- Festival time. Stepmother prioritises her daughter, not wanting men to see beautiful Yeh-Shen first. Told her to stay home and watch fruit trees.
- Yeh-Shen speaks to bone of fish and asks for clothing – cloak of kingfisher feathers and golden shoes. Spirit of the fish told her not to lose her shoes, she thanks it and goes to festival. Turns heads.
- She overhears her stepsister identifying her.
- Yeh-Shen ran and lost one shoe, clothes turned back into rags. Only had one golden shoe left. Stepmother found her with her arms wrapped around a fruit tree.
- Villager found the shoe and sold it to a merchant who presented it to the king of a nearby kingdom. The king was entranced by it and wanted to find its owner. It was too small.
- King planned to place shoe in pavilion to attract the right woman to it. Yeh-Shen snuck out to the pavilion. Hoped to return both shoes to the spirit of the fish.
- King was going to throw her into prison, but saw her beauty and they followed her home. The king asked her to try on the shoes and transformed into a heavenly being and the king realises he's in love.
- She marries the king, forbids her to see her stepmother and stepsister because they were unkind to her. Not long after her stepmother and stepsister are killed in a shower of flying stones.

VICTOR H. MAIR, 2005

- Story was passed down of a tribal leader named Wu
- He married two wives, one died, leaving a daughter Yexian
- She was intelligent, good at working gold and this is why her father loved her
- Wu died and her step-mother abused her
- She caught a fish and helped it grow
- Fish would greet her
- Step-mother came to find out about the fish and deceived Yexian so she could use her clothes
- Stepmother killed the fish and made a meal out of it
- Yexian cried, person arrives from the sky and consoled her, telling her that praying to the bones would grant wishes
- Community festival – Yexian left to guard the fruit trees, but instead went in a blouse of kingfisher feathers and golden slippers.
- Younger sister notices Yexian and Yexian runs away, losing a slipper.
- Tribal member found the slipper and sold it to the military island kingdom of Tuohan. When anyone tried on the slipper, it would shrink an inch.
- The ruler ordered the finder of the shoe imprisoned, instructions to search everywhere for the matching slipper. They searched and found Yexian, she makes a grand entrance in her beautiful clothes.
- She tells the king everything and he takes her and the fish bones with him.
- The stepmother and daughter were killed by flying stones, they were buried in a stone pit and it was called Tomb of the Repentant Women.
- Yexian is made primary wife.
- The king uses the fish bones for unlimited treasures after a year, they no longer responded. He buried them on the seashore but they were washed away by the tide.
- This story told by a former servant of the narrator's household, who was originally from a tribal community in Yongzhou

SYMBOLS AND MOTIFS

YEXIAN
YEH-HSIEN
YEH SHEN:
means Leaf Limit

FESTIVAL:
"The isolation of long winters within closed doors, the ceaseless toil of the rest of the year, with brief interludes in spring and autumn which betrothal and marriage festivals were held, made up an existence so precarious that every member of the community must necessarily have devoted his full attention to the business of being." (Edwards, 1974, p.4) As a result, the festival likely occurred around December.

FISH SKELETON:
Many folktales contain bones and in this context, they may represent fertility or a new life. Could the fish have represented her father? Confucius supported ancestor veneration and fish was used for food but also symbolic of good fortune and represented in art and culture.

SHOES:
It is unlikely the original people wore shoes, but shamans wore straw sandals. However, in Vietnam, women would craft their own shoes to fit their feet perfectly (Beauchamp, p. 458).
It appears that the tradition of footbinding was not practiced until after the story was written down and was intended to shape the feet for dancing (like en pointe) (Szczepanski, 2019).

ROCKFALL:
Mair suggests that throwing rocks is a behaviour more likely to be in Middle-Eastern cultures, rather than Chinese. In the story, it's almost an after-thought to push a moral lesson about the stepmother's behaviour. Particularly since where they died became a sacred place where young men could wish for wives. The violence, according to Beauchamp, could also be representative of a political statement about an insurrection during this period.

CAVES:

They were referred to as cave dwellers, but 'cave' might be a colloquialism for a villager. The story itself has Yexian in rooms of her home. According to a legend, outlined in Mair, "scholars who were fleeing from the 'burning of books' carried out by the First Emperor of the Qin dynasty (221-207BCE sought refuge in this place (Hunan). Upon arrival, they deposited the texts they brought with them in a cave on the mountain. These writings (which survived nowhere else) were later discovered by people who had wandered into the cave. Because of this legend, the name Youyang came to signify rare and old books from far away" (2005, p. 364).

POTTERY:

"Pottery is usually regarded in China as man's work," but it is unknown whether the Indigenous women of the area did pottery (Waley, p. 230). According to Mair, the verb used to describe what Xexian was good at "may have been...spinning gold thread" (2005, p. 366).

CARP:

Beauchamp's research asserts that a gold and red carp "ties together Hindu, Zhuang, and Han narratives and traditions" (2010, p. 455).

CLOAK:

What Yexian put on has been described as a 'cloak' or a 'blouse' made of halcyon (kingfisher) feathers. According to Jackson, the Chinese have been using kingfisher feathers for thousands of years to "denote status. wealth and royalty." According to Beauchamp, her "finery ...is not a foreign costume but the wonderful revelation of her native dress, her "true" identity," (2010, p. 253).

DUNG HEAP:

It would have been a "...filthy place that would have included garbage, excrement, and most likely ashes" (Mair, 2005, p. 366). This is a possible source for the ashes that later appear in European versions.

MARRIAGE:

According to Encyclopaedia.com, during this period "...the marriage institution evolved into a complex structure...if the parents were dead, the intention of marriage had to be reported to their spirits in the ancestral hall and at a shrine at home." It is unlikely the stepmother would not have made efforts on Yexian's behalf to help her arrange marriage.

The Lost Shoe

YEXIAN ADAPTED BY ALYSSA CURTAYNE

I lost my shoe. Who loses a shoe? And a magical one at that. To tell you what happened, I will need to go back to the beginning so you know how I came to possess shoes in the first place. Nobody wears shoes in our village. Our feet are wide, flat and covered in a layer of grime which is almost impossible to get off. Every day ends with wiping the grit off our feet before we lay down to sleep. In the winter, we wrap our feet in a layer of cloth, but that's only to protect them from the cold. Only the wealthy wear shoes, and despite my father being chief of our village, shoes were not for people like me.

My shoes were gold. Real gold soles, they felt heavy in my hands, but to wear them, I felt like I could float with the clouds. The tops were woven like the scales of a fish, glittering like sunlight on the water. When I ran my hand across them, it was like I was feeling my friend once more. I expected my feet to feel squeezed when I had them on, but they fit me just perfectly, even magically resizing to suit my hardened soles. Sometimes I get out my remaining shoe and hold it tightly to me when I sleep at night, without its mate, the spirit of my friend no longer speaks to me either in its bones or through my shoe. But even still, the remaining one left gives me comfort, for I am an orphan.

My mother, died just after I was born and although I never knew her, my father created a shrine for her in the gardens and planted an orange tree to remember her. At times, I would sit in front of the shrine and imagine what it may be like to have a a mother who cared for me, and who wanted what was best. I imagined what she might look like, how she would smile at me, how we might cook together over the hearth, or teach me how to be a mother. When my father remarried, I think in some way he hoped his new wife would raise me as she would have, but they soon had their own child and maternal instinct only goes so far. If he had survived the last pestilence maybe my life would be different, but here I am, a girl, waiting for something to change, hoping that somehow, I won't feel so alone in the world.

Every morning my stepmother threw a bucket at me and sent me off to the furthest well to get fresh water. Sometimes she would make my sister follow me to be sure I went to the furthest one, not the well close to our village, with the freshest, cleanest water. But the one that was found up a steep cliff, through a valley, and in the midst of a dense forest. My sister would report everything I had done back to her. I imagine if my father had lived, my sister and I would have been friends, but she did everything her mother said, or she took a beating, as I did.

When I returned from the well, my stepmother would put me to work scrubbing and cleaning everything in our home, my father's home, then sending me back into the forest to collect firewood until my arms ached and my body was bleeding from cuts and scrapes. My bed was the only place in the world I had to myself and it was there I hid my shoe.

One day my stepmother and sister had gone to visit relatives and would be gone all day, she barked her orders to do all of my usual jobs, bringing out the switch just in case I had any thoughts of disobeying her. But I longed for nothing more than a bath. My menstruation began and while she threw me some cloths to help stem the flow, she did nothing more to help me. I could smell the dank and odorous smell that lingered like a vapour.

I did my household chores as quickly as possible then with my buckets set out for the river. The river was in the valley on the way to the deep well and the moment I arrived, I stripped everything off and scrubbed them clean on the banks then set them to dry in the overhanging branches. Goosebumps covered my skin, but my body melted into the stream, surrendering to its coolness. I floated a while, my hair loose and free for the first time in months. I remember looking at the blue of the sky, clouds drifting into shapes as the current moved me slowly away from my village. I didn't think much of it when it brushed past me the first time, but it tickled so that I sat up and saw a tiny fish, no bigger than my finger gazing up at me. It had round, golden eyes and a red fin and whiskers that curled like my father's moustache.

"Hello there," I said. Its scales were so tiny then and felt smooth under my fingers. The fish seemed to be talking as if I knew what it was saying. It is a strange memory and hard to describe what I felt, but I knew that this fish was my friend and companion. I sat in the water a while talking to it and letting my body be cleansed. After dressing, I scooped the fish up in my palms and placed it into one of the buckets, and returned home. I found a small bowl and placed it inside and fed it with scraps of food whenever I could. Over time, my fish grew, and grew and each time I replaced the bowl with a bigger one until it was too hard to hide it from my sister and stepmother. I needed to find a new home for it.

In the cliff face on my walk to the deep pond was a cave, and inside that cave was a pond as long as two men. Plants grew down the walls and a little waterfall trickled fresh water into it. There was a small, sandy bank at the edge and not even my sister knew about this place, I had been careful to not go there when I knew she was following. It was the perfect home for my friend. I rose before the bucket hit me that morning and went to the pond in the darkness.

The trickling of the waterfall calmed me as I checked one last time to make sure I was not followed. There was a smattering of filtered sunlight but otherwise it was the perfect home for my friend. I dropped it into the water, and it swam in great circles in its new space. I sat on my knees on the sand and talked to it before leaving a morsel of food and leaving to continue my duties for the day. Every day I got the opportunity to return, I brought food and to talk, not ever staying long and always dutifully checking if I was followed. My fish friend grew bigger and bigger until it filled the length of the pond itself.

At the start of winter, my stepmother asked me to do something she never had done before.

“Come here,” she commanded. “Take off your filthy cloak,” she grabbed me roughly. I remember having bruises on my arms from this interaction. “Put this on and go into the next village. I need rhubarb.” She put me in her old jacket and pushed me out with a few coins. “Be respectful,” she said.

The journey was at least half a day there and back and while her demeanour seemed unusual, I’m unsurprised by her idiosyncrasies and strange behaviour anymore. I completed the task and it was nearly dark when I returned.

But it wasn’t until the next day that I could go to see my friend. The cave seemed quieter than usual, and I called my greetings quietly. But it didn’t swim out to meet me or pillow its head upon the bank, just its head, eyes vacant and whiskers lifeless. It’s then I cried, for the first time in my life, I sobbed so deeply that I vomited onto the sandbank. I could barely breathe, my tears pouring in streams for my mother, my father, my fish friend, and myself. One of my tears fell into the pond and I watched as it rippled across to the other side where a light appeared. The light grew larger until I turned to see a being descend from the sky.

It floated above the water and told me of my stepmother's betrayal. How she had disguised herself in my cloak, slipped a dagger up her sleeve, and then brought it down when my fish came out to greet her. She had taken my fish, the being said, and had fed it to my sister. I vomited again. Feeling the emptiness that one feels after the death of a beloved.

I felt a hand on my shoulder, "Do not cry," the being said, "your fish is filled with a magical spirit."

I sat up, and looked at their kindly face, coarse clothes, and long, white hair, that fell in waves down their shoulders.

"Retrieve the bones of your fish from the dung heap and should you ever desire anything, kneel before them and your wish shall be granted," they said. Before I could ask them any more questions, the being rose back into the sky and I was left alone again.

Upon my return, my stepmother said nothing and neither did I, but I imagine she saw my swollen face and red eyes. I continued my chores as if nothing had happened. Every time I went to the dung heap to drop off ashes, food scraps, or broken pottery, I would retrieve some of the bones. After a while I found them all and took them to the cave pond where I shed more tears as I washed my friend's remains, bone by bone. I then placed them in my most precious cloth and put them underneath my pillow. I didn't ask for much from the spirit of the bones. Food mostly, sometimes fresh cloths for my menstruation, things my stepmother and sister could not see or find.

The end of winter was a time of celebration in the village; the people of the neighbouring villages come together to reconnect, tell stories, trade, and arrange marriages between young people. My sister had been eager to strike a match this year and as a result, I was forbidden from going. My stepmother had asked the ancestors for a blessing for my sister and clearly didn't want potential suitors to confuse me with her.

"You are to protect the fruit trees from thieves," my stepmother instructed as she and my sister went on the path through to the meeting place. I diligently put my head down and continued cleaning the hearth. As soon as they were out of sight, I knelt before my bones, looking at my grubby skin, the dirt under my nails, and my tattered clothing. The bath in the river was a distant memory and I knew at once what I desired from the spirit of the bones of my beloved friend.

In an instant I was transformed, my skin was clean, my hair was clean and styled and I was cloaked in a gown of iridescent kingfisher feathers. On my feet were the most perfect pair of shoes, gold like my fish's eyes and scales stitched from the finest hand covered the top and a solid base that felt like I was walking on air. I felt the essence of the spirit of the bones radiating from the centre of my being. With thanks to my friend, I made my way to the festival.

Far from disappearing into the shadows, I let myself be seen and admired by many an eye as I strolled through the festival, smiling and greeting them. I heard them whisper about me and my extraordinary clothing, and I took it all in, filling me with a sense of purpose and place in the world. I passed by my sister who told her mother "Doesn't that look like our Yexian?" The blood rushed from my veins and before my stepmother could look at me, I made my way to the exit as calmly as I could before taking heel down the hill towards home. Not being accustomed to wearing shoes, one came off on the way and this is why you will find me here, with my body wrapped around the orange tree in my tattered clothing, sobbing over my lost magical, golden shoe.

Of course, I still have the other one, but my shimmering clothing is gone. Wait! I hear something. It is my stepmother checking in on me. She's gone now. I return to my fish bones and kneel before them telling them my woes as I used to tell my fish friend. But they are silent. What have I done? Without the other shoe, the spirit of my friend is silent. I hug my bones and the remaining shoe to my chest and fall into a restless sleep.

The bucket misses in the morning and I rise and begin my daily chores. She never misses, perhaps she secured a match for my sister and is in a good mood. I shrug and return to my chores, the festival a distant memory. I return to hiding from my stepmother's unpredictability. Days turn into weeks and still, the spirit of the bones remains silent.

A whisper runs through the village. The king of a nearby island is on his way to the village, seeking a golden shoe. The king arrives in the village to a great ceremony, his men, knock down doors and arrest people if they refuse him entry. I hide the bones and the shoe and assume the demeanour of a mouse. He soon arrives at our home, and both my sister and her mother put on the shoe the king has bought with him, and the moment they do, the shoe shrinks in size. A soldier grabs me roughly and puts me in front of the king, my foot outstretched. The moment the shoe touches my toes, it glows and moulds itself to my foot. I see the look of recognition in my sister's eyes and the hate and resentment in my stepmother's. She kneels at the king's feet and he kicks her away.

"Where is the other shoe?" he says gruffly, not taking his eyes away from my foot.

I stand and retrieve it from my bed, putting it on my other foot. Instantly, my cloak of iridescent blue returns, and I can feel the essence of my friend once again. I feel radiant and look hopefully at the king, but instead of admiration, he demands to know how I came across such powerful magic. I reluctantly tell him about my fish, its death, the visit from the spirit, and how whatever I desire can be created. He commands that I hand over the bones and he takes me and my shoes and the bones back to his island.

My fish bones make him incredibly rich and as a result, he makes me his chief wife. I am abundant with more food and clothes and comfort than I've ever experienced, but my new husband is ruthless and shows no kindness. Word comes that my stepmother and sister are killed in a landslide and I weep for what could have been, for my solitude, for my fish, for my father, and for my cloak and shoes my new husband has hidden. And my life returns to a routine of submission and hopelessness.

It is a night like any other when I hear a whisper from outside my window. I wrap a shawl around my shoulders, dismiss my servants, and follow the whisper down to the river. My bare feet sink into the soft sand on the shoreline. The closer I come, the louder the voice gets, it's my fish friend. I stand ankle-deep in the tepid water seeking their friendly face, their comfort, but it is blackness. The whisper calls me to the shore. I kneel down and begin digging, sand gathering under my nails. The bones are still wrapped in my father's cloth and I peel it open. The bones sigh.

"Lay down beside me," it says.

Somehow, I know that this is how it ends, I know that I cannot continue in the life that has been chosen for me. For the first time since my father died, I get to make my own choice. I don't notice the water rising, but finally, the spirit of my friend and I are together again.

https://www.erinclaireillustration.com/

A child, lost and alone
Devoid of a belonging
Finds in darkness
A friend, a fish

Severed from the true heart
Disconnected from spirit
Her friend brings hope
Her friend brings peace

Violence undeserving
Betrayal of a mother
Grief comes quickly
Despair returns

Buried deep in the bones
Ancient magic awakens
Seeking the truth
Of time and place

Hope revived in dazzling,
Iridescent blue, gold shoe
Takes flight, not right
Betrayed again.

Bones call her lonely heart
A girl, no longer hoping
Tide out to sea
Tide out to sea

Final thoughts

The intention of this project was not to interpret the story, but to provide a summary of the source material so readers can make their own interpretations. The Beauchamp article proports that "c. 850 Yexian story is an original creation of the Zhuang who combined ideas from their own traditions and experiences with motifs from more widely circulated stories" (Beauchamp, 2010, p. 469) and contains a comprehensive analysis of the Zhuang people of Guangxi Province during the Tang Dynasty, the influence of Hindu mythology and the significance of the objects of the time. I encourage you to seek it out for yourself.

Instead, use this material to inspire your own stories, your own performances and your understanding of Cinderella as different from the passive, weakened heroine we have seen throughout the 20th century. "The Yexian story is not one of a culturally impoverished heroine, but of a girl with cultural resources who subverts attempts to change her status to one resembling a household slave"
Beauchamp, 2010, p. 459.

May the story of Yexian never be forgotten, a story of a kind talented and intelligent young woman, abandoned and alone, who found hope and friendship in the animate and inanimate world, "it is with a female identity, heritage, and knowledge that she rescues herself," (Beauchamp, 2010, p. 743).

NOTE: There are multiple Chinese versions of Yexian available, but only very few academic translations into English. As a non-native speaker, I have done my best to compile this with the three translations as outlined above. They have been the primary sources for this document and are in the bibliography. Unfortunately, I was unable to source the 1932 Jameson text but have referenced it in the Bibliography.

Anderson, G. (2000). Fairytale in the Ancient World, Routledge, London, viewed 30 July 2023, <https://search.ebscohost.com/login.aspx?direct=true&db=e000xww&AN=60882&site=eds-live&scope=site>.

Beauchamp, F. (2010). Asian Origins of Cinderella: The Zhuang Storyteller of Guangxi. Oral Tradition, 25(2). doi:https://doi.org/10.1353/ort.2010.0023.

Edwards, E. D. (1937). Chinese prose literature of the T`ang period, A.D. 618-906 / by E.D. Edwards Arthur Probsthain London

Heiner, H.A., (2012). Cinderella Tales from around the world : Fairy Tales, Myths, Legends and other Tales with Cinderellas. Nashville: Surlalune Press. https://surlalunefairytales.com/bookstore.html

Jameson, R. D. & Chung-kuo wen hua hsueh yuan. (1932). Three lectures on Chinese folklore, delivered before the convocation of the North China Union Language School, March and April, 1932, by R. D. Jameson North China Union Language School, cooperating with California College in China Peiping (Peking) China.

Louie, A.-L. (1982). Yeh-Shen a Cinderella Story from China.

Mair, V. (2005). 54. The First Recorded Cinderella Story. In: Mair, V., Steinhardt, N. and Goldin, P. ed. Hawai'i Reader in Traditional Chinese Culture. Honolulu: University of Hawaii Press, pp. 363-367. https://doi.org/10.1515/9780824852351-061

Reed, C. E., & Duan, C. (2003). A Tang miscellany: an introduction to Youyang zazu. New York, Peter Lang.

Szczepanski, K. (2019). Imperial China's Foot-Binding Tradition. [online] ThoughtCo. Available at: https://www.thoughtco.com/the-history-of-foot-binding-in-china-195228.

Waley, A. (1947). 'The Chinese Cinderella story', Folklore, 58(1), pp. 226–238. doi:10.1080/0015587x.1947.9717844.

www.encyclopedia.com. (n.d.). Wedding Customs | Encyclopedia.com. [online] Available at: https://www.encyclopedia.com/history/news-wires-white-papers-and-books/wedding-customs.

Zhang, J. (2020). 'Rediscovering the Brothers Grimm of China: Lin Lan', Journal of American Folklore, 133(529), pp. 285–306. doi:10.5406/jamerfolk.133.529.0285.

Cover image and art piece: ©2023 Erin-Claire Barrow
Other images by DejaVu Designs, Anjali Mehta, Vector Tradition, PicturePartners, Tui Brightwell's Images, Layer-lab, angychan0982 via Canva.com
Author photo: Zest Photography

Alyssa has been teaching for 30 years. She has a Graduate Diplor in Creative Writing from Deaki University, is a member of the Australian Fairy Tale Society, a oral storyteller (specialising in fc and fairy tales) is a former journa and sub-editor, a former Englis teacher and a lover of the ability stories to transform and transpo us into our shared humanity.

www.ingramcontent.com/pod-product-compliance
Lightning Source LLC
Chambersburg PA
CBHW060528310726
48982CB00002B/465

* 9 7 8 0 6 4 5 8 7 4 2 9 7 *